Cheng Ho

Written by
JULIA MARSHALL
&
Illustrated by
LAURA DE LA MARE

HOOD HOOD BOOKS

Cheng Ho

Copyright © Hood Hood Books 1996

Hood Hood Books
29 Bolingbroke Grove
London SW11 6EJ

British Library Cataloguing-in-Publication Data
A catalogue record for this book is available from the British Library

ISBN 1 900251 22 1

Origination by : Fine Line Graphics, London
Printed by: IPH, Egypt

Cheng Ho

Every night the boy dreamed that the soldiers would come. He imagined them galloping over the rolling green hills that surrounded his village, wading through the rice paddies and the fields of white and purple poppies. Everyone would run and hide, but the soldiers would find them, wounding and killing them with their bows and arrows and their sharpened swords. He understood the dream. His father had told him all about it. He had sat him down and said, "Now listen carefully my son. I want to tell you how we came to be living in this village among the rolling green hills." And the boy, who was almost ten years old, sat very still and listened to what his father had to say.

"I have given you the name Ma Ho. Ma is my name, the name of your grandfather and his father before him. When people hear that name they know that we are Muslims and worship one God. Our ancestors came to China with the Mongol warriors who swept across Asia, conquering as they came. For almost a hundred years they ruled China, but ten years before you were born, Hung Wu, who is now Emperor of China, rebelled against the Mongols and won. He is all-powerful, our Emperor, and his word is law. To disobey him means certain death. I have heard stories, my son, stories of great cruelty and we must all be careful. We have been settled in China for some generations now and our loyalties are towards China; but our Emperor is worried that our Mongol blood may be a threat to his power. He has ordered his soldiers to go to certain areas of China where most of the descendants of the Mongols have settled and to wound or kill all men and boys who disobey. It may be that these soldiers will come here to where we live. So we must be watchful, my son."

His father laid a hand on the boy's head, as if to protect him from harm. Ma Ho looked at his father and saw that his proud, high forehead was now creased with wrinkles. "My son, we are not a rich family, we have very few possessions, but I have travelled to Mecca and brought back valuable knowledge which I have passed on to you. You speak good Arabic and know the customs of foreign lands. You are a clever boy, my son, and I pray to God that this will protect you from harm."

And then, very early one morning, just as the sun was rising, the Emperor's soldiers came. At first, only the drumming of the horses hooves could be heard echoing in the still air. But then there were shouts and cries, the clash of swords and the singing of arrows released from bows. Ma Ho woke and felt a wave of terror move through his body. His father pulled him to his feet. "Run, my boy, run and hide. I am an old man, they may not harm me, but you must flee." He kissed his son on the forehead, knowing that it might be for the last time. "I will pray for you," he whispered as Ma Ho set off, his heart beating with fear.

Ma Ho ran faster than he had ever run. He blocked all thoughts from his mind and felt only the racing of his blood through his body as his heart beat harder and harder. At last, exhausted, he crouched under a tree. The soldiers passed by and he thought, he hoped, he may have escaped. But one of the soldiers glanced in his direction and let out a great cry.

"Look!" he shouted, "under that tree." It was too late to run. Ma Ho rose to his feet and stood very still. The soldier who had spotted him, prodded him with his sword. "A fine looking boy this," he said. "Let's take him and question him. If he proves to have some intelligence, we'll present him to the Emperor. A boy like this would make a good servant at the Imperial Court." The other soldiers agreed and Ma Ho was swept up and carried away. He

was roughly handled, but he survived and the day came when he was presented at court along with several other boys.

Ma Ho stood tall and straight while the Duke Yan, uncle to the heir to the throne, walked past, inspecting the prisoners. He came to a halt in front of Ma Ho. "Hmm," he said and lifted Ma Ho's chin with his hand, peering into his eyes. "This boy looks a good, strong specimen." He questioned Ma Ho and to everything that was asked of him, the boy answered clearly and intelligently. The Duke smiled. "A very fine boy," he said. "I will take him and have him trained. I believe he would make a good soldier."

And so it was that Ma Ho joined the Duke's retinue. By the time he was twenty he had become a fearless soldier who had fought many battles against China's enemies outside the Great Wall. The enemy were terrified when they saw Ma Ho: he had grown from a small boy into a giant more than seven feet tall, as large and broad as a great tree, with glaring eyes and a voice that boomed like thunder. Anyone seeing him for the first time might think that he was no mere man, but the god of war himself!

Meanwhile, Duke Yan was plotting against his own nephew who had become Emperor at the age of sixteen. He seized his chance and, in a great battle, took the throne for himself and became the Emperor Yung Lo, the all-powerful ruler of China. Ma Ho was his most prized soldier and he decided now to reward him

for his loyalty. Ma Ho was given the new surname of Cheng - which means three jewels - and was placed at the head of thousands of men. One day the Emperor summoned Cheng Ho before him. The great giant of a man bowed low before his Emperor who rustled the exquisitely embroidered silk of his magnificent robes.

"You have been a good and loyal servant," he said to Cheng Ho, "and I have great plans for you. I think it is about time that the world was reminded of the greatness of China. Indeed, I think it only fair that those people unfortunate enough to inhabit barbarian lands be treated to a visit from our magnificent land, so that they may learn about our superior culture and customs." The Emperor paused and took a deep breath, letting it out slowly. Cheng Ho waited patiently for what he would say next. "I am having ships built, many large ships and I have chosen you, Cheng Ho, to lead an expedition to foreign lands. I will furnish you with various articles of Chinese craftsmanship, embroidered silk, porcelain, incense and such like for you to offer as gifts to these foreign people. Of course, you understand that I do not mean you to trade with these people. As great an Emperor as I would not stoop to the lowly business of money-making. But if any of these foreigners should want to present the Emperor of the greatest land with tribute to express their admiration, you would not want

to refuse them that pleasure. Indeed, I will graciously receive any-thing they have to offer." The Emperor made a grand gesture with one hand and gave a small half smile. "And there is another small matter, Cheng Ho. I wish you to get rid of that pirate, Chen Tsu-i, who has made Palembang his base and guards the Strait of Malacca, allowing no ship to pass without trading with him or being robbed. He has become too powerful and I want him stopped. See that it is done."

It was a hot summer that year in 1405 when Cheng Ho prepared to set sail on the first of his voyages. There were three hundred and seventeen ships waiting in the harbour. Some of them were great treasure junks, almost four hundred feet long, filled with rich silks, sweet-smelling incense and delicately painted porcelain. Then there were the war ships - smaller and easier to manoeuvre - armoured with iron sheets and fitted with giant crossbows and guns. The ships were coated with lime that made them as white as snow so that they looked like vast ghost ships. Great eyes were painted on the hulls so that it looked as though they could see where they were going; and the war ships were decorated with tiger heads to frighten the enemy. Before going into battle, the sailors put on whiskered tiger masks. Some people, seeing these strange white ghosts ridden by wild animals moving towards them would flee in terror rather than stand and fight.

At dawn Cheng Ho climbed aboard his flagship, the Star Raft, and along with twenty-seven thousand men, set sail for the dangerous waters of the Indian Ocean. He did not know then that this was only the first of seven voyages that he would make. He would spend the next twenty-eight years of his life sailing the seas, visiting thirty-seven foreign lands all the way to India and Africa, covering a wider expanse of water than anyone in the world before him.

As the ships neared Palembang, the seat of the powerful Chen Tsu-i, Cheng Ho summoned one of his men. "I have an important task for you," he said. The man nodded gravely and listened to what his leader had to say. "I'm going to send you ashore. I want you and a few other men whom I will personally select, to go ashore and infiltrate the house of Chen Tsu-i. Find out all you can about his strategies, his army and his war ships. On my return journey we will use this information to defeat him. Go now and good luck to you."

Cheng Ho left his secret agents behind and, avoiding any confrontation with the famous pirate, sailed past Palembang, making his way towards India. He navigated with the help of charts drawn on silk, compasses made of needles that floated on water, and astronomers who spent many hours studying the stars.

The journey was sometimes dangerous with great storms whipping the waves so that they rose up like huge mountains, threatening to crush the ships beneath them. During a hurricane, Cheng Ho believed his life had come to an end, but he knelt and prayed to God to save him and his men. Then all at once a red light appeared out of the dark, floating above him on the mast of his ship. Suddenly, the waters became calm and Cheng Ho and his men were saved.

They sailed on, all the way to Calicut on the south-west coast of India which was the home of the great Sea King, Malayalam. The skin of the Sea King and all his chiefs was covered by a white paste made from ox-dung and, to Cheng Ho and his men, they presented a strange picture. But they began to unload the treasure from their ships and the smile of the Sea King grew wider and wider as he saw the magnificent riches the Chinese had brought with them. For many months goods were exchanged and

then, before they left, the Sea King presented Cheng Ho with a great golden girdle, studded with precious jewels, as a token of his admiration for the great Chinese Emperor, Yung Lo. Ambassadors were sent back to pay their respects to the Emperor in person.

At last Cheng Ho set sail for China. He was eager to see his home again, but he still had the pirate, Chen Tsu-i, to deal with. When he reached Palembang he prepared his ships for war and the sailors put on their tiger masks. He demanded Chen Tsu-i's surrender. The pirate at once gave in, but the secret agents who Cheng Ho had left behind warned him not to believe Chen Tsu-i. They knew that he had secretly prepared for attack and, sure enough, a great and fierce battle took place. Cheng Ho's men fired flaming arrows from their crossbows, setting fire to the enemy's ships. Five thousand pirates were killed and Chen Tsu-i was captured and taken back to China.

The Emperor Yung Lo was satisfied. He smiled his small half-smile, accepted the gifts Cheng Ho had brought back from foreign lands and immediately had Chen Tsu-i, the famous pirate King, executed. Now ships would be able to pass through the straits safely.

Cheng Ho was hardly given any time to rest before he was ordered to set out once again on a voyage that was to last another two years. This time Cheng Ho and his fleet sailed to the

15

Indonesian islands. As he approached them he was amazed by their beauty - they looked like floating green shells in the deep blue of the sea. He decided to land at Java, but he and his men were met by a hoard of fierce inhabitants carrying knives. Java was divided into two, the East and the West, and the East King and the West King were fighting among themselves for control of the island. Before Cheng Ho and his men knew what was happening, they were attacked and a hundred and seventy of their men were slaughtered by the soldiers of the West King. The West King feared Cheng Ho, recognising what a brave soldier and a great leader he was. He offered him sixty thousand pieces of gold as compensation for the death of his men, but Cheng Ho refused. He would not give in to such bribery. He defeated the West King in battle and set up the East King as ruler, restoring peace to the beautiful island of Java and winning the respect and love of its people. They named Cheng Ho Sanbao and promised that he would live forever in their memories.

Once again there was no rest for Cheng Ho. Almost as soon as he returned, he had to make ready for a third voyage. He had to use his skills as a soldier when he and his men were attacked at midnight by the King of Ceylon with fifty thousand troops. The King was after the wonderful treasure that he had seen the Chinese bringing from their great treasure junks. Cheng Ho defeated the King and saved the Chinese riches before he returned to China. This time the Emperor allowed him over a year to prepare for his next voyage when he would sail all the way to Arabia. He stopped at nineteen different countries on the way and they all sent ambassadors bearing exotic and precious gifts to offer to the great Emperor of China. The King of Bengal sent the most wonderful present of all - a giraffe.

The Emperor sat on his throne, dressed in his magnificent robes, surrounded by courtiers waiting for Cheng Ho to bring the foreign ambassadors with their gifts. His eyes grew larger as he saw the giraffe approaching. He had never seen such a strange animal and he was not sure whether he approved of such an unusual creature. He drew Cheng Ho to one side and said, "What is this animal who is fifteen feet high with the body of a deer and the tail of an ox? Why is it covered in those spots the colour of a purple mist? From what cursed land does it come?" The Emperor frowned, and Cheng Ho thought quickly. He bowed low before his Emperor and said, "Why, that is a unicorn, your Excellency." For once the Emperor smiled widely. In China the unicorn only appeared to rulers of perfect virtue. The gift of a unicorn was the highest compliment of all.

The next three voyages of Cheng Ho were all to the coast of Africa. The foreign ambassadors had to be escorted home and the

Emperor had acquired a taste for exotic animals. Not only giraffes, but elephants, camels, rhinoceroses and ostriches filled the holds of the treasure junks. But the Emperor Yung Lo was now an old man. He sickened and died, and with his death the golden age of seafaring came to an end. Never again would such glorious white ships with red sails and painted eyes sail the seas of the Indian Ocean. Cheng Ho himself was now over sixty. It was not long before he too died, and although the records of his journey were destroyed by those who were jealous of his great adventures, he would always live on in the minds of the people he had visited.

Stories of the wonderful voyages of this great giant of a man were passed on from generation to generation. Temples were built in his honour, and to this day the Chinese people of Indonesia go every year to the Tajue temple to pay their respects to Cheng Ho on the anniversary of his first visit to their land. Elsewhere in the world it is claimed by some that Cheng Ho - or Mao Sanbao's - heroic and dazzling feats became the basis of the stories and adventures of Sindbad the Sailor.

HEROES FROM THE EAST